LUCY RUNS AWAY

Also by Catherine Storr:

Lucy

LUCY
RUNS
AWAY

By Catherine Storr

Illustrated by
Victoria de Larrea

PRENTICE-HALL, INC.
ENGLEWOOD CLIFFS, N.J.

LUCY RUNS AWAY by Catherine Storr

First published in the U.S.A. by Prentice-Hall, Inc.,
Englewood Cliffs, N.J., 1969

First published in Great Britain by The Bodley Head, 1962

© by Catherine Storr, 1962

© by Prentice-Hall, Inc., 1969, for illustrations in this edition

13-541235-8

Library of Congress Catalog Card Number: 75-81385

Printed in the United States of America • J

Prentice-Hall International, Inc., London
Prentice-Hall of Australia, Pty. Ltd., Sydney
Prentice-Hall of Canada, Ltd., Toronto
Prentice-Hall of India Private Ltd., New Delhi
Prentice-Hall of Japan, Inc., Tokyo

To Emma

Contents

LUCY RUNS AWAY

CHAPTER ONE

"One day I shall run away," Lucy said.

"Where to?" Jane asked.

"I don't know where to. And I wouldn't tell you if I did," Lucy said. "You'd come after me and bring me back."

"I wouldn't! I'd let you stay wherever you were. But I expect mother would want you back again."

"She wouldn't be able to find me."

"She'd get the police."

"I'd disguise myself," Lucy said.

"The police would see through your disguise. They're cleverer than you," Jane said.

1

"Why do you want to run away?" Caroline asked.

"People in books do. Then they have adventures. I want adventures," said Lucy.

"What sort of adventures?"

"Rescuing people. Finding buried treasure. Meeting pirates. Something exciting."

"You've been watching too much television," Jane said. "Things like that don't happen to us."

"They don't happen to you, but they will to me."

"Why to you?"

"Because I shall run away."

"You won't really," Jane said. "You'll talk about it, but you'll never do it."

"Never do what? What won't Lucy do?" Lucy's mother asked.

"Won't run away."

"I hope she won't."

"I will," said Lucy.

"Not just yet," her mother said. "Wait till you're a little older."

"How old?"

"Don't run away before you're twelve," her mother said.

"I can't wait till I'm twelve!" Lucy cried. "Then I'll be too old for adventures!"

"Eleven and a half, then."

"Ten," Lucy said.

"That's only three months!" Caroline said.

"Then I'll go in three months!"

"No, Lucy. Please!" her mother said.

"I'll wait till I'm ten. Or nearly. Then I shall run away."

"Won't you ever come back?" asked Caroline.

"Yes. When I've had some adventures. Not before."

"Don't go too far. I shall be anxious about you," her mother said.

"You needn't be. I can look after myself."

"You haven't enough money," Jane said.

"I've got some Christmas money saved up. And my pocket money."

"Ten cents a week!" Jane said, and she laughed.

"I will go," Lucy said to herself. "Jane and Caroline are silly. They don't want adventures. I do. When I'm ten I shall take my money and I shall go. I shall run away."

Chapter Two

It was summer. Lucy's house didn't have a proper garden, only a small paved space round which her mother grew daffodils in the spring, wallflowers and forget-me-nots in the summer, and dahlias in the autumn. Now the wallflowers were straggling and the forget-me-nots had lost their color and began to look like weeds. The yard was dusty and smelled of cities and smoke and hot paving stones. Lucy sat in a deck chair with her eyes shut, and pretended she was the mysterious outlaw having an adventure.

He was sitting on the back of his coal-black horse, Midnight, on the top of a hill. Far below him a herd of cattle grazed peacefully and he could see the winding white ribbon of the road that led to the town. He could see the stagecoach lumbering sleepily along, drawn by two fat gray horses. It had come from the gold mine on the other side of the hill, and it was carrying boxes of gold nuggets to the bank in the township. Suddenly there was a crack! crack! and three masked bandits rode out of the bushes and held up the coach. The driver was pulled off his seat and tied up, the two guards were overpowered, and the frightened passengers were huddled in the road, begging for mercy. The bandits quickly unloaded the boxes of gold and piled them high beside the coach. The mysterious outlaw put his rifle to his shoulder and squinted down the barrel. Slowly he squeezed the trigger. Crack! A bandit dropped the gun with which he had been terrorizing the passengers. He squeezed again. Crack! Another bandit, carrying a heavy case of nuggets, fell to the ground with a bullet in his leg. The third saw that the game was up. He jumped on his horse and rode off. The passengers untied the coachman and the guards, the coach was re-loaded, and started slowly on its way. It was safe, thanks to the mysterious outlaw of the prairie.

No one in the township knew who it was who kept law and order for them, defeated the bandits and outwitted the Indians. They were as much frightened of the lonely figure seen galloping across the prairie on his jet-black horse, as they were of their better-known enemies. Only Lucy knew from what dangers he had saved them, and how often. They owed their safety, their wealth, their houses, their lives to him.

Lucy opened her eyes. After the wide distances of the imaginary prairie, the garden looked very small, very sooty. A prowling cat came along the other side of the trellis that divided Lucy's garden from Mrs. Martin's, next door. It half-shut its eyes and gave Lucy an insolent look. Lucy pointed her second and third fingers at it and her thumb pressed the trigger.

"Bang! Bang! You're dead," said Lucy softly.

The cat sat down and began to wash itself. It had a bib that should have been white, and paws which needed washing very badly.

From inside the house Lucy could hear Caroline practicing the piano. She was learning to play "Lavender's Blue" with both hands. Each time the left hand had to come in with a chord, there was a long pause while Caroline found the notes. Sometimes she found the wrong ones. It was not a cheerful sound.

"I'm tired of streets and houses! I'm tired of little gardens and cats and Jane and Caroline. I'm tired of being a little girl at home! Nothing exciting ever happens here," thought Lucy.

"In six weeks I shall be ten. I shall save up my money and then I shall go and seek my fortune. I shall run away," said Lucy.

CHAPTER THREE

On one of the kitchen shelves stood a fat china pig, dark blue with white spots, in which Lucy kept the pocket money that she didn't spend. She got it down and, with the help of a knife blade, emptied the coins out of the wide slot in his back.

"You're rich," Caroline said, looking enviously at all the pennies and nickels and the occasional dime spread out on the kitchen table.

"Help me to count," Lucy asked.

"Seventy-eight cents. What a lot! What are you going to do with it, Lucy?"

"I won't tell you. It's a secret."

"Honestly, I won't tell."

"No," said Lucy.

"I can guess," Caroline said. "You won't get far with that. Why it wouldn't even get you into the country."

"If I walked it would."

"Stupid! It'd take you days and days to walk into the country. You'd get tired long before you got there, and you'd have to have somewhere to sleep at night."

"I could sleep in a field."

"In the town? There wouldn't be any fields. You'd have to pay to stay in someone's house. You haven't got nearly enough."

"I've got a lot more upstairs in my bedroom. I've got an envelope with my Christmas money in it."

"How much?"

"I won't tell you."

"You don't know."

Lucy went upstairs and looked in the envelope. Some of the silver money was large and some was small.

"Mother, look how much money I have here," Lucy said, "a fifty cent piece, two quarters, five nickels, five dimes and twelve pennies. A dollar eighty-seven."

"It's a great deal," her mother said. "You must be a very good saver."

"It's from my last birthday and Christmas. I bought a basket for my bicycle but nothing else. There wasn't anything I wanted," said Lucy.

"So now you are rich."

"What could I do to get thirteen cents, to make it two whole dollars?"

"Clean my best shoes," said Lucy's mother. "With white polish and a clean rag, please."

"I've got two dollars," Lucy said to Jane that night.

"I don't believe it! What are you going to spend it on?" Jane asked.

"I'm not going to spend it. Not yet."

"You could buy a space-gun with an electrical death-ray attachment," Caroline said.

"You could buy a set of twenty-four crayons, all different," said Jane.

"I don't want to," Lucy said. To herself she said, "I'm going to have adventures with my money. I'm going to run away."

Chapter Four

Every night in bed Lucy thought about running away.

She knew she couldn't run to a desolate prairie where there would be highwaymen and Red Indians, and cowboys and stagecoaches and sheriffs. They weren't around nowadays. Nor was William Tell, nor Robin Hood, nor Bonnie Prince Charlie, nor any of the really exciting things in history that other luckier children could have gotten mixed up with ages ago. Life today was dull. One went to school, one came home, one quarreled with

14

one's sisters. Only the children in books and plays had adventures with smugglers and spies and bandits.

"Have you ever seen a pirate?" she asked her father at breakfast.

"Not to recognize. Not one I could be sure was a pirate."

"Or a bandit?"

"Silly! We don't have bandits in England," Jane said.

"Don't be so positive. Look at my newspaper," her father said.

"TRAIN BANDITS ROB MAIL. GUARD TIED UP IN HIS OWN BRACES," the headlines of the newspaper shouted.

"Real bandits? Did they steal anything?"

"Thousands of dollars."

"Do we have smugglers, too?"

"They row secret boats to deserted beaches at night, with brandy and lace," Caroline said.

"They hide hundreds of watches in their boots and underclothes and bring them over the sea from other countries," Jane said.

"Why from over the sea?"

"Because England is an island. If you went far enough in any one direction from here, you would come to the sea. That's what being an island means."

"Could I get to the sea?" Lucy wondered. At the sea she would find smugglers, perhaps pirates if there were still any. Once, when she was too young to remember, the family had enjoyed a holiday by the sea. "Do you remember Haven?" Jane and Caroline asked each other sometimes. "Lucy can't, she was too little. Do you remember the sand? Do you remember the rock father dived off? The caves? The harbor? Do you remember Haven?" they said.

"Are there smugglers at Haven?" Lucy asked.

"I expect so. There certainly were not long ago. I can imagine the caves coming in very handy, and some of those empty beaches, too. I'm sure the harbor-master at Haven knows more than he ever lets on," Lucy's father said.

16

"Couldn't we go there again?"

"Sometime. It's a long journey."

"In a train? Can you get there by train?"

"Yes. There's a train that goes all the way from here. We'll go one summer, Lucy. The railway station is right on the edge of the harbor. You can see the sea as you arrive."

"Does it cost a lot? More than two dollars?"

"Yes. Even for you it would cost more than that."

"Do boats go to other countries from there?"

"Certainly. But you'll have to stay in England for a little longer."

"Bandits on trains. Smugglers on the beaches. I shall go to Haven," Lucy thought. "The mysterious outlaw would find adventures in a place like that."

CHAPTER FIVE

As the summer went on, Lucy saved her pennies. But she still hadn't enough money to run far away by train. She would have to think of something else.

"Shall I run away on a bicycle?" Lucy wondered.

She got her bicycle out of the shed in the garden, and pumped up its tires. The basket on the handlebars was small and would not hold much. Some sandwiches and a raincoat would be all she would be able to carry.

"How many miles would I be able to go on my bicycle?" she asked Jane.

"Goodness, I don't know! About two, I should think."

"How much is once around the block?"

"I've no idea. Ask father."

"About a quarter of a mile," Lucy's father said. "But that's only a guess."

"So how many would make a whole mile?"

"Don't you know *that*?" Caroline said, but her father said, "four."

"And how many would make two miles?"

"Eight."

Lucy packed her bicycle basket with books. If she was going to practice she must be properly loaded.

"Where are you going with all those books?" Caroline asked.

"Are you running away? You're not ten yet," Jane said.

"I'm just going to ride around the block," Lucy said.

She set off. Once around the block seemed a very short way. The pavement was uneven and bumped her up and down, but there was also a place where the ground sloped down-hill and she could coast.

"Whoa!" said Lucy to her bicycle. The mysterious outlaw sat back in his saddle and let Midnight, his coal-black horse, gallop at his own pace.

She went around the block a second time.

"Twice more and it will be a mile," she said.

The third time she went around, some workmen who were building a wall whistled at her.

"Practicing for a race?" one of them called.

"No," Lucy shouted back, but she felt a little embarrassed at going past them a fourth time.

"Warm work!" they said as she went by, and it certainly was very hot. Lucy's face prickled with heat and her legs ached. The uphill part of her journey seemed suddenly much steeper than before and the bumpy bits of pavement were actually uncomfortable.

"I'm aching with tiredness. The mysterious outlaw was too stiff to walk after being on horseback all day," Lucy thought.

The fifth and sixth and seventh rounds were bad, but the eighth was terrible. She practically fell off outside her own gate.

"Lucy, what have you been doing?" her mother asked. "You're scarlet and dripping!"

"I've ridden two miles. I really can't walk. I've got saddle sores," said the mysterious outlaw.

"You poor silly girl! On a day like this? Go upstairs and have a cool bath and I'll bring you an icy drink."

"I can't run away on my bicycle," Lucy thought, lying back in a refreshing bath. "I'd never get anywhere. I shall have to think of something else."

"How far can I run?" she asked her mother later. They were having tea and there were big black juicy cherries piled in a bowl.

"In this weather or in the winter?"

"Any weather."

"I should think half a mile if you didn't run fast."

Lucy felt depressed. Half a mile would not get her into the country.

"How far could I walk?"

"If you rested along the way I don't see why you shouldn't walk for three or four miles without being exhausted."

"I'll try tomorrow," Lucy thought. "Not today, I'm too tired. And I won't walk round and round the block, or the workmen will laugh at me."

The next day after school she walked down the hill to the High Street. On the corner of the High Street was a signpost. One arm, pointing to the right, had a great many names on it; the arm pointing to the left just said "To the North," and this was the sign that Lucy liked best.

"To the North," she thought and turned left. She thought of icebergs and frozen seas, snow-covered continents and the top of the world. She would go to the North for her practice running away.

She passed the dairy on the corner. Mr. Jones was standing at his door.

"Good afternoon to you, Lucy!" Mr. Jones called out. "How are you doing, and your sisters, too?"

"Very well, thank you."

She passed the fishstore.

"Hullo!" Sandy called from behind his counter. "Going far?"

"I don't know yet."

She passed the help-yourself super-market where you could buy practically everything.

"Why, it's Lucy!" said Mrs. Greenwood, stepping out of the NO ENTRANCE door. "Where are you off to?"

"Just out."

"Aren't you energetic? Nice to see you. Have a good time."

She passed the butcher's. Mr. Orlik and his son were pulling the shades down over the windows to keep their meat cool and fresh.

"Good evening," Mr. Orlik said. "Hot, isn't it?"

"Very hot."

"Going for a nice walk?"

"Yes," Lucy said, but she didn't feel like going for a nice walk at all. Everything was spoiled. How could she run away and be a mysterious outlaw when someone recognized her and spoke to her at every other step? It was too bad. And she was tired already and there were hundreds more shops to pass. Lucy turned around and went home.

Chapter Six

Lucy had her birthday. She had presents and a cake. Her godmother sent her two dollars. She was ten. She had waited three months and kept her promise to her mother. Now she had enough money to get to the sea by train and the time had come for her to go.

For three days after her birthday she considered her plans. She would go to the railway station by bus: she would go early so as not to miss the train and still avoid all the friends and neighbors who would stop her and talk. But she would go after breakfast because if she were missing for that meal the search for her would begin before she had time to get anywhere. Also it would be as well to start her adventures with plenty of food inside her.

On the evening of the third day Lucy packed her satchel. She put in a flashlight, a purse containing all her money, a cardigan, a copy of *Robinson Crusoe*, the mysterious outlaw's black mask, pistols and holster belt, and some food. Two bananas and some choco-late, and as much bread and cheese as she could remove from the pantry without her mother noticing.

"After all, I'd be eating it if I was at home, it's not like stealing," she thought.

She hid the satchel under her chest-of-drawers.

"Goodnight, my big girl. How does it feel to be ten and three days?" her mother asked.

"Better than being nine. What are we going to do tomorrow?"

"Nothing special. Jane needs some new shoes. I must make your winter pajamas and get your blazer from the cleaners. School next week," her mother said, "goodnight!"

Downstairs, Lucy's mother said to her husband, "I'm glad to say Lucy seems to have forgotten all about her plan to run away when she was ten. I was half expecting her to disappear the day after her birthday, but she hasn't mentioned running away for weeks. It must have gone out of her head."

"Good," said Lucy's father.

Upstairs, Lucy remembered something. She got out of bed and packed three clean handkerchiefs next to *Robinson Crusoe*.

The next morning Lucy came down early to breakfast. There was no time to be lost.

"Goodness, you're eating a lot!" Jane said.

"It's only my third slice of bread and syrup!"

"But you had eggs and bacon first, and your cereal. You'll have to undo your belt."

Indeed it was already uncomfortably tight.

"I'm very glad if Lucy eats a good breakfast," her mother said. "She's a skinny creature. She could use a bit more weight."

"But not all at once," Jane said.

"Perhaps she's got a tapeworm," Caroline
said, interested. "You get them in under-
cooked pork and they live in your stomach
and eat up all your food as it goes down so
that you don't get any, and you get thinner
and thinner and the tapeworm gets longer and

28

longer, so you're always hungry. But it's only the head that counts," she added vaguely.

"Please, Caroline! Not at breakfast!"

"I thought you'd like to know. Probably you ought to take Lucy to the doctor. She's got an unnatural appetite."

"I'm all right," Lucy said. "I'm hungry, that's all."

She had to force down the last mouthfuls of bread. She was afraid she might be going to have a pain which would have been a waste of time, but fortunately it turned out to be a false alarm.

"Where are you going, Lucy?"

"Upstairs to get something. Then out."

"Are you going to play in the lane?"

"I might. Or I might go down to the shops."

"Most of them won't be open yet."

"I could look in the windows. Or I might go round to see Elizabeth."

"Very well."

"If she asks me to lunch, may I stay?"

"If her mother agrees."

"And tea?"

"No, you can't live in Mrs. Sedgewick's house. Besides I must have you to measure the pajamas against. You must be home by half-past two, Lucy."

"By half-past two I'll be miles away," Lucy thought.

She went upstairs to look for her satchel. She went into the closet and got down her raincoat, too.

"Is that you, Lucy? Goodbye!" her mother called from the kitchen.

"Goodbye!"

"What on earth are you wearing a raincoat for?" Jane asked. "It isn't going to rain."

"What have you got in your satchel? It's busting full," Caroline said.

"Just like Lucy," Jane said. "Only in her it's breakfast!"

They laughed so much that they didn't notice that Lucy hadn't answered their questions. She let herself out of the front door and shut it behind her.

It was almost too easy. It didn't seem right that one could run away with so little trouble. Lucy felt that she should have escaped at night, in stockinged feet, with a dark lantern. Midnight, her horse, should have been tethered to a post outside the house, state police should be waiting to question her at the frontier. It should have been a dark, dangerous journey. Could one expect to have adventures by simply walking out of the house after breakfast, on a bright sunny morning, with one's mother comfortably calling, "Goodbye"?

"Other people might think he was just an ordinary sort of person going out for a walk," Lucy said to herself. "But really the mysterious outlaw was leaving his home forever."

Chapter Seven

The mysterious outlaw strode down the hill toward the bus stop. It was very early. One or two women with baskets on their arms were buying groceries: only the shops that sold food were open. Lucy peered round the corner at Mr. Jones' dairy: the door was shut and the blind was pulled down inside it, but over the tins in the window Lucy could see Mr. Jones busily shaping small golden bricks out of a huge mound of shining butter. She went past the windows very quickly. Mr. Jones did not look up.

The bus stop was a hundred yards down the High Street. Two or three people were waiting there, and Lucy hurried on to join them. She passed the bank, which was shut, and Woolworth's, and the chemist and the stationer and the toyshop, all shut. The bakery was open: it smelled so deliciously of new bread that Lucy almost felt hungry again. She slowed down to get as much of the smell as she could. There was no one inside that she knew, nor in the Post Office next door. There were no cars outside the big garage which came next: the gas stations were all deserted. No one had spoken to her, no one had stopped her. Lucy began to feel safe.

"Concealed by his heavy disguise, the mysterious outlaw passed unnoticed through the crowds," she thought.

She passed the big row of apartments and the candy store. Just by the bus stop was the movie house, and it was now that Lucy saw, standing just by the entrance, in front of the pictures out of the film, the large dark-blue shape of a policeman.

The policeman was just standing, as police-men do. He looked up the road and down the road and he looked at the two people waiting for the bus.

"At the frontier the state police waited. But the mysterious outlaw would escape from their clutches again," Lucy thought.

She did not want to join the line under the policeman's nose. She had better not be seen or remembered. She stood in the door-way of the candy store and waited for the bus to arrive.

"I hope it comes soon," Lucy thought.

Two more people came to stand at the bus stop. The policeman looked at them without interest.

"He is waiting for the mysterious outlaw," Lucy thought.

There was a slot machine in the doorway of the candy store which sold cigarettes and bars of chocolate. Lucy had no money to spare, but to pass the time she pulled at all the drawers. One of them came out a little further than the others, and to encourage it,

Lucy kicked the machine gently. The drawer did not move, but something inside clanked loudly and there was a rattle of coins.

The policeman looked around.

Lucy hid behind the machine.

A badly dented nickel had fallen out into the returned coins tray. Lucy put out a doubtful hand and picked it up.

The policeman left the movie house entrance and strolled down past the candy store.

Lucy made herself thin. As thin as the one shiny silver leg that held the thick interesting part of the machine.

The policeman strolled back again and glanced at the colored pictures outside the theater.

"Busy with their own affairs, the state police did not notice the mysterious outlaw creeping nearer and nearer to the frontier," Lucy thought.

She felt uncomfortable about the nickel. Was it stealing to take a rejected coin that she hadn't put in herself? Had she done something terrible to the machine when she kicked it? She would have liked to kick it again to see what would happen next, but it was too noisy and dangerous an experiment.

"All right, I'll give it back," Lucy said.

She put the battered nickel into the slot. There was another immense clatter and the drawer which had stuck shot out. Under Lucy's hand lay a bar of milk chocolate.

The policeman turned sharply.

On the other side of the slot machine the mysterious outlaw stood very still.

The line at the bus stop was now quite long. Lucy wondered if there would be room for her on the bus when it came. A politely dressed man with a bowler hat and an umbrella was arguing with a stout woman as to who had gotten there first.

The policeman looked at the arguing people. He looked back at the slot machine where everything was perfectly quiet. The stout woman's voice was getting louder. He stepped forward toward the line.

The bus rounded the corner and came tearing down the hill.

Lucy reached round the slot machine and picked up the bar of chocolate. She saw the bus pull up suddenly and the people scrambling to get on. The conductor was counting them, the bus was very full. At the last moment the mysterious outlaw emerged from his hiding place, dashed across the pavement and threw himself onto the platform of the bus.

"And that's the last one," the conductor said. The bus gathered speed in a moment. As it hurtled off Lucy saw the policeman go up to the slot machine and kick it, much harder than she had ever done.

"And so the mysterious outlaw, having out-witted the police and crossed the frontier, entered the unknown country," she said to herself.

Chapter Eight

At the station the mysterious outlaw had no difficulties. There were a great many people standing and walking and hurrying, going away in trains and arriving back in trains; sitting on benches, buying newspapers, drinking cups of tea and eating sandwiches. Lucy felt sure no one would notice her. She saw one or two policemen standing about, but apparently they were not looking for anyone in particular. If they had been told to arrest a slot machine thief or an outlaw leaving his home town, surely they wouldn't stand talking to each other in such an easy way? However,

Lucy kept as far away from them as she could. Porters told her where to go, kind travelers standing in endless lines helped her to buy the right sort of ticket. She found the platform from which her train would leave and when it came she climbed in.

"None of the passengers knew that, sitting silently among them, was the mysterious outlaw himself," Lucy said.

The train hummed and shook and talked to itself in a sing-song voice as it panted through miles and miles and miles of green and brown countryside. It was very warm and

rather stuffy in Lucy's compartment, because the lady in the purple hat in the far corner wouldn't have the window open. She said if it was opened even an inch she would have such terrible pains in her face she wouldn't be able to sleep all night. Lucy had read her book, she had looked out of the window, she had eaten her lunch. The journey seemed to be going on forever. Lucy didn't have a watch and she had already asked the time from the man opposite so often that he had sounded quite annoyed. Haven must be hundreds of miles away. Lucy began to wonder if she would ever get there. Presently she slept.

The train stopped several times and half woke her up. She knew that people got out of the carriage and other people got in, but she was too sleepy to take much notice. When she was at last fully awake, the compartment was half empty. The lady in the purple hat had gone and the man with the watch had gone and so had the mother and father with a baby and a dog. Two new people had come in and the only person who had traveled all the way from London with Lucy was an elderly woman with a great many newspapers.

"You've had a long sleep," she said to Lucy.

"Have I? Where are we now?"

"We've just passed Kingsbridge."

"Is that near Haven?"

"Not very far. We've only about another half-hour before we're there."

This was good news. Lucy looked out of the window and saw quite a new sort of country. There were heathery hills and deep valleys: great lumps of gray stone lay about on the hillsides, as if a giant had thrown them there. It was quite different from the gentler, rolling, green country in which Lucy had gone to sleep. This was much more sudden. But there was no sea.

Lucy went out into the corridor to stretch her legs and to look for the sea. But the country on the other side of the train was just the same as she had already seen. At the end of the corridor was an unsafe, shaky-looking piece of floor which led into the next carriage. Lucy peered round, and saw the freight car. It was not very full. There were several cartons, two bicycles, some suitcases and one corded trunk. In a sort of pen, barred off from the main part of the car, were two calves on some tired-looking straw. They made mooing noises when they saw Lucy looking at them and stuck their soft black noses sadly against

the bars. Lucy was sorry that she had nothing to give them. She stroked their rough foreheads and let them lick her hands, but she could not comfort them as she would have liked.

The guard came into the car as she was talking to them.

"Seeing to my calves?" he said.

He had a red friendly face and a soft West Country voice.

"They're not very happy," Lucy said.

"Missing their mothers," he said. "Like you would if you'd just left yours."

Lucy wondered if she did. Not as badly as the calves, anyhow. She said, "I wouldn't. I'm not a baby."

"But you wouldn't like to be on this train all alone, without your mother, would you now?"

"I am."

"What, m'dear?"

"My mother isn't on this train. I'm running away."

"From your school?" the guard said. His fat friendly face looked puzzled and anxious.

"No," Lucy said airily. "From home."

"You shouldn't do that," the guard said. "Your mother will worry about you. She'll want to know where you are."

"She won't worry. I told her I would run away when I was ten, and now I am ten and I have."

"She isn't unkind to you now, is she?"

"No."

"Anyone unkind to you at home?"

"Yes, sometimes. Horrible," Lucy said. thinking of Jane and Caroline.

"It's all right, m'dear," the guard said suddenly. "I'll see they don't get you back. The Society. That's what you want."

"What? What society?"

"N.S.P.C.C. National Society for the Prevention of Cruelty to Children. Ah! Wonderful work they do for little girls with bad homes like yourself."

"What do they do with them?"

"Find them new homes where they're properly looked after, m'dear. You leave it to me."

Lucy did not want to leave it to the guard. She did not want a new home. She said quickly, "Don't you ever have bandits on this train?"

"Bandits, m'dear? What would they be on this train for, then?"

"To steal your mailbags for thousands of dollars. Haven't you ever been tied up and gagged?"

"No."

"Not once?"

"Not that I can remember," the guard said. He still looked puzzled.

"How far are you traveling on this train, m'dear?" he asked.

"To Haven. Are we nearly there?"

"Very nearly at Haven now, m'dear. Don't you worry what to do when we get there. I'll see the man from the Society takes you somewhere safe."

The train stopped at a small station. Two young men in very short shorts came and took the bicycles out of the car. The train

47

lingered a few moments and then went on.

"I think I'll go back to my carriage, thank you very much," Lucy said.

"You can stay here if you want," the friendly guard said.

"No, thank you. Goodbye!"

"Cheerio! I'll look for you at Haven."

But when the train at last reached Haven, Lucy was out of the compartment, past the ticket-collector and running down the road to the town before the friendly guard had moved from his seat. To be put into a safe home by a man from the Society! That was not the sort of thing that happened to the mysterious outlaw!

CHAPTER NINE

In Haven the tide was high. Blue water filled the harbor basin, and all the little boats, some with folded sails and some without, rocked gently at their moorings. On several of the tall masts, seagulls were pretending to be carved out of painted wood. Others sat on the water as comfortably as we sit on cushions. A small boy of about Lucy's age was rowing a dinghy in and out between the larger boats. A motor boat with FERRY written on the flag painted at her bow was puttering around a more distant wharf.

Lucy was tired and terribly thirsty. Even

before she put more distance between herself and the friendly guard, she had to have a
drink. She bought a carton of orange squash
from a shop that sold everything from vege-
tables to bull's-eyes, and sat on a large stone
toadstool bench on the edge of the wharf,
sucking a deliciously cold sweet drink through

a straw, and wondering what to do next. She had been in the train the whole afternoon. Although it wasn't even beginning to get dark, she could see from the way the shadows were sloping and from the families who passed her toadstool, that it was the time when people shut up their shops and tied up their boats and took their tired babies home to bed. Lucy began to think about bed. She didn't mean to spend her money on a real one. If it was fine, and it looked fine, she meant to sleep out. But she couldn't sleep out in the town. She supposed she could walk until she came out of the town into country, but who knew how far that would be?

She looked around. There were buildings all around the little harbor and climbing right up the steep hill above it. Outside the harbor was a wide sweep of water and then more land, perhaps a different country. It had a sandy beach with only one or two houses behind it and a great deal of grass and trees. It looked much more like country than this side. Lucy wondered how she could reach it. She looked at the little boats below her, she looked at the ferryboat which had just come round the further wharf, she looked at the big boat near the railway line, she looked at the road leading from the railway station, down which she had just come. There was a handful of people walking down it. Two women, five schoolchildren, a tall man in a bright yellow sweater, a fat red-faced man in a dark uniform and a peaked cap.

It was the friendly guard.

Lucy did not wait. She took her satchel, dropped the empty orange carton into a convenient litterbasket and ran. She threaded her way between the crowds of holiday-makers toward the far wharf where the ferryboat was waiting. She ran down the stone steps just as the boatman was untying the rope and stepping in himself. He gave her a hand and she threw herself in. The engine revved up with a roar and the boat hurried out of the harbor. As they rounded the far wharf, Lucy saw the fat friendly guard look over the edge of the harbor wall as if he expected to see Lucy floating in the water below, among the little rocking boats.

CHAPTER TEN

The ferryboat took Lucy straight over the water to the distant sandy shore she had seen from Haven. The journey was windy, cool, choppy and wonderful. Lucy enjoyed every moment. She thought it was the best five cents' worth she had ever had. If it hadn't been for the thought of the friendly guard waiting for her on Haven wharf, she would have gone straight back again.

Instead she was helped out on the farther shore into soft wet sand that sucked at her shoes. The rest of the boat's passengers straggled off toward the houses and a road. Lucy sat on the sand and took her shoes and socks off. Then she turned her back on the houses and began to walk along the shore in the opposite direction.

She saw now that she was at the sea end of a great river. It was across the wide mouth of the river that the ferry had brought her. On the side she had come from was Haven, which she now saw was a not very large town crowded round the harbor: behind it and on

each side were green fields and trees. On this side of the river there were hills and stretches of soft loose sand, with a forest of tall thin grasses growing out of it. Ahead of Lucy, but a very long way ahead, the river suddenly opened out into an immense sheet of water which reached right away until it touched the sky.

"That is the sea," Lucy thought.

She would have liked to get to the sea. The river was all very well, but she wanted the open sea. She walked toward it for what seemed a very long time. The sand was very soft and her legs grew very tired. If she walked down by the river it was wet as well as soft and her feet sank right in. If she walked up above the beach, the grass stung her legs and she had to go up a great many small sandy mountains and down a great many sandy valleys. And all the time the tide was falling: the river by her side got narrower and narrower and the beach of soft rippled sand on each side of it became wider. The sky faded to a pale blue and the little clouds were tinged with pink. A fresh salty wind blew up from the sea, and the colors of the water and the grass and the sand lost their brightness.

Lucy was very tired; she was hungry and rather cold.

"Perhaps I shouldn't have run away," she thought. "Perhaps I'll go back home tomorrow."

Then she had a really miserable idea. "I haven't enough money to get back!"

She sat down in the shelter of a sand dune and cried a little. Then she thought how Jane and Caroline would laugh at her. "You're too little to run away," they had said. "You'll talk about it, but you'll never do it."

"Well, I have done it." Lucy said to herself. "Even if I'm miserable and hungry and cold, I have run away and I've run a very long way away, too. The mysterious outlaw said he would reach the sea, and of course he did."

It occurred to her that she needn't be hungry and cold as well as miserable. She took off her raincoat, buttoned herself into the cardigan she had packed in her satchel, and put the coat on top of that. She ate some bread, the last banana and some chocolate. She had finished the cheese in the train.

"I'll just have a little rest and then I'll go on till I reach the sea," Lucy thought.

She made a hollow for herself in the warm dry sand. Now that she had eaten she felt more comfortable inside and not nearly so cold. She was very tired indeed. Very soon she slept.

Chapter Eleven

Bright sun and the screaming seagulls woke Lucy up.

"Where am I?" she asked. Then she remembered. "I ran away. I am almost at the sea."

She felt quite different. Still hungry, but warm and brave. The river had filled up again in the night and the sun was shining on the blue dancing water. It didn't matter that she hadn't enough money to get home. It didn't matter that she was eating her last piece of bread and the last crumb of slot-machine chocolate. She had outwitted the state police, and escaped from the friendly guard and his Society. She had run away nearly to the sea.

The mysterious outlaw had proved his worth again.

"I am going to reach the sea," said Lucy.

She started to walk toward it. The sand was still soft underfoot and the walking was tiresome, but Lucy felt strong. The sun grew warm and she took off first her coat and then her cardigan. It didn't seem worth undressing any more, so by the time she reached the long curved beach, with rocks and firm dry sand which faced the open sea, she was extremely hot.

"Bother!" Lucy said. "I forgot to bring a bathing suit."

But on second thought it didn't seem to matter. There was nobody about. She hadn't seen a single person since she woke that morning. Even the ferry wasn't working yet. Lucy took off everything she had on and went cautiously into the water.

It was a wonderful beach. The waves were gentle and curled like white lace around her toes. When she sat down they cooled her hot sticky back. When she lay down they played with her, pushing her this way and that, splashing her hot sticky face with fine spray, running away and pretending they had left her high and dry in the sand, then dashing back again to roll her over and over.

"This is what I came for," Lucy said. "It was worth running away just for this. This is my adventure."

She had just dressed again and was trying to dry her hair on a clean pocket handkerchief, when she saw that there was another person on the beach. A man, quite old, in a gray

flannel suit and a straw hat was coming past the rock where Lucy was sitting. He had a bundle wrapped in a towel under his arm.

"Best time of the morning for a bathe," he said as he passed her.

"It's lovely!" Lucy agreed.

"Often come down here?"

"Not very often," Lucy said cautiously.

"Thought I hadn't seen you before," the old man said triumphantly, and went on down the beach.

He undressed very neatly and quickly right in the middle of the sand. When he took off his hat, Lucy saw that he had a bald pink top to his head surrounded by tufts of white hair. But he didn't go at once into the water. Instead he did exercises, stretching and touching his toes, and running on the spot, and swinging his arms round like a windmill. He looked very funny all alone in the middle of the beach working so hard; but Lucy got tired of waiting for him to go into the sea. She started to walk up the beach toward a signboard on the grass, to see if it might give her any ideas about what she should do next. If there was nothing interesting to be seen she thought she would go back to Haven and find a boat on which she could stow away to get to Africa or America. Or perhaps she would go further along the cliff and try to find a smuggler's cave or some pirates. The signboard said:

DANGER
Strong currents make this beach dangerous at falling tides. Bathers are advised not to swim out and to keep to the left side of the beach. In case of difficulty sound alarm at the side of lifebelt holder.

The lifebelt holder was immediately below the notice. The lifebelt hung on a hook, with a great coil of rope inside it. The alarm was a handle at one side. Lucy touched the handle and it said, CLICK, once, very loudly.

How dull! But perhaps it was a good thing that Lucy hadn't swum out and had been on the LEFT side of the beach and that the tide hadn't been a falling one. Lucy looked back at the beach.

The tide was certainly falling now. There was a great deal more sand uncovered than when she had been playing with the waves. The little pile that was the old man's gray flannel suit and straw hat were now a long way from the foam at the edge of the sea.

Quite far beyond where the gentle little waves were breaking, Lucy could see a bald pink head surrounded by tufts of white hair. It seemed to be swimming out to sea.

As she looked, it disappeared. Not behind a wave, but just down into the sea. The old man must be diving.

When he came up again he waved both his hands. Lucy politely waved back.

The head disappeared again.

Lucy waited.

The head came up again. Very faintly, carried by the salt wind, the sound came to Lucy's ears. 'Help! Help! HELP!'

The mysterious outlaw knew exactly what to do. He turned the handle of the alarm rattle. It made a splendid noise.

Chapter Twelve

When all the fuss was over—and it was a great fuss—and the hundreds of people who came running at the sound of the alarm had sent a man out on the end of a rope, and had brought the old man in from the sea, and had laid him on the sand and brought him back to life: when they had wrapped him in blankets, and poured brandy down his throat and taken him off to hospital in a fast bell-ringing ambulance: when all this had happened, at first terrifyingly slowly and then very quickly indeed, everyone wanted to know all about

64

Lucy. They asked her who she was and where she had come from and what she was doing and why: and before she knew what was happening, she had been thanked and cried over by the old man's wife and daughter, congratulated by the Mayor of Haven, photographed by the local newspaper men, and was in a train under special care of a guard—a different one —bound for London.

"But I'm running away!" she said. But nobody listened. And remembering that she had no food left, and not much money, and that she had, anyhow, had an adventure, she went.

"Please don't run away again. I was frightfully worried," her mother said.

"Lucy, you mustn't run away," her father said. "We didn't sleep at all last night. The police were looking for you everywhere."

"I slept. Out-of-doors, in the sand dunes," Lucy said.

"Wait till you're older," her mother said. "Promise me you won't do it again."

"But mother, I got to the sea! I escaped from the guard! I saved the old man's life!"

"Promise," her mother said.

"But mother, I had real adventures! I was quite safe!" said Lucy.

"You might not be lucky another time. Promise me, Lucy."

"All right. I promise. Until I'm about twelve, at any rate."

———

"You see?" she said to Jane and Caroline. "I didn't just talk about it. I did run away."

"I didn't believe you'd really gone till I heard mother telling the policeman," Jane said.

"Was the old man frightfully grateful?" Caroline asked.

"You are lucky to have been to Haven. *We* haven't been to Haven for years."

"Will you get a medal for saving him?"

"Where will you go next time?"

"She can't run away again. She promised mother."

"Only till I'm twelve," Lucy said. "I've got to start saving up again."

"Where will you go when you're twelve?"

"I haven't decided. I might go to Africa or America. Africa probably."

"You'll never get enough money for that," Caroline said.

"You wouldn't go so far away," Jane said.

"You said I wouldn't run away at all," Lucy said. "But I did."

She left Jane and Caroline and went to sit in the garden. It was still warm in the sun, and now the dahlias made a bright ring round the small, sooty paved space. Lucy shut her eyes.

The mysterious outlaw stood on a towering cliff high above a raging river. The banks had burst, and a sheet of tumbling, foam-sprinkled water covered what had once been a peaceful valley. Suddenly, among the waves he saw a human head: above the roar he heard a cry for help. It was the sheriff, Good Jim Courage, who had been swept unawares into the flood.

Kicking off his boots, the outlaw dived from the crag, a hundred feet down into the torrent below. With a few powerful strokes he reached Good Jim and dragged him unconscious to land. Hours later the sheriff would recover his senses and find himself safe, without knowing who his rescuer had been. The mysterious outlaw was at work again.